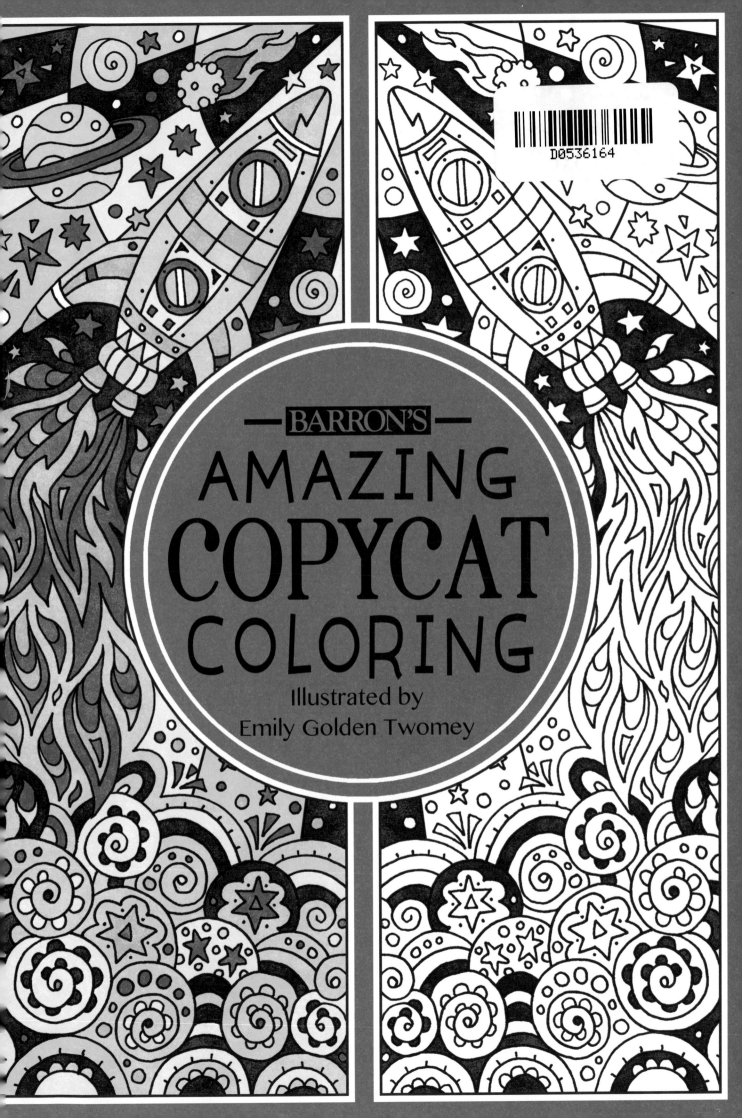

BARRON'S

AMAZING COPYCAT COLORING

Illustrated by
Emily Golden Twomey

CAN YOU COMPLETE THESE AMAZING PICTURES? YOU CAN FOLLOW THE COLOR GUIDES EXACTLY AS THEY ARE, OR USE YOUR OWN COLORS TO CREATE SOMETHING NEW. IT'S TIME TO MAKE A MASTERPIECE.

THE PAGES IN THIS
BOOK WERE COLORED
AND COMPLETED BY

....

First edition for the United States and Canada published in 2015 by Barron's Educational Series, Inc.

First published in 2014 by Buster Books, an imprint of
Michael O'Mara Books Limited, 9 Lion Yard, Tremadoc Road, London SW4 7NQ

Copyright © 2014 Buster Books

With thanks to Amy Clayton

All inquiries should be addressed to:
Barron's Educational Series, Inc.
250 Wireless Boulevard, Hauppauge, New York 11788
www.barronseduc.com

ISBN: 978-1-4380-0635-2

Product conforms to all applicable CPSC and CPSIA 2008 standards. No lead or phthalate hazard.

Manufactured by Wing King Tong, Shenzhen, Guangdong, China

Date of manufacture: December 2014

9 8 7 6 5 4 3 2 1